North Carolina
Facts and Symbols

by
Shelley Swanson Sateren

Consultant:
Jennifer Bennett, Vice President
Professional Educators of North Carolina

Hilltop Books
an imprint of Capstone Press
Mankato, Minnesota

Hilltop Books are published by Capstone Press
818 North Willow Street, Mankato, Minnesota 56001
http://www.capstone-press.com

Library of Congress Cataloging-in-Publication Data
Sateren, Shelley Swanson.
     North Carolina facts and symbols/by Shelley Swanson Sateren.
     p. cm.—(The states and their symbols)
     Includes bibliographical references and index.
     Summary: Presents information about the state of North Carolina, its nickname, flag, motto,
and emblems.
     ISBN 0-7368-0381-5
     1. Emblems, State—North Carolina—Juvenile literature. [1. Emblems, State—North
Carolina. 2. North Carolina.] I. Title. II. Series.
CR203.N76S27 2000
975.6—dc21   99-31820
                                                                                                                          CIP

Editorial Credits
Christy Steele, editor; Heather Kindseth, cover designer; Linda Clavel, illustrator;
   Kimberly Danger, photo researcher

Photo Credits
Corbis, 6
John Elk III, 22 (bottom)
Kate Boykin, 10
One Mile Up, Inc., 8, 10 (inset)
Photo Network/Bill Terry, 12
Robert McCaw, cover
Transparencies Inc./J. Faircloth, 22 (top); J.E. Glenn, 22 (middle)
Visuals Unlimited/Jeff Greenberg, 14; Al Simpson, 16; Gary W. Carter, 18;
   Joe McDonald, 20

Table of Contents

Fast Facts

Capital: Raleigh is North Carolina's capital.

Largest City: Charlotte is North Carolina's largest city. About 469,600 people live in Charlotte.

Size: North Carolina covers 52,672 square miles (136,420 square kilometers). It is the 28th largest state.

Location: North Carolina is in the southeastern United States.

Population: 7,546,493 people live in North Carolina (U.S. Census Bureau, 1998 estimate).

Statehood: North Carolina became the 12th state on November 21, 1789.

Natural Resources: North Carolinians mine crushed stone, phosphate rock, and clay.

Manufactured Goods: North Carolinians make textiles, wooden furniture, and machines.

Crops: North Carolina farmers grow cotton, tobacco, and soybeans. Livestock farmers raise cattle, sheep, and pigs.

State Name and Nickname

English settlers named the Carolina colony in honor of King Charles I of England. Carolana means Land of Charles in Latin. The spelling changed over time.

One popular story from the Civil War (1861–1865) explains the nickname Tar Heel State. During a hard battle, North Carolinians fought alone while other Southern troops fled. After the battle, a Virginian soldier tried to make fun of the North Carolinian soldiers. He asked if there was any tar left in North Carolina. The state was known for producing tar. One North Carolinian soldier said that Confederate President Jefferson Davis bought all the tar. He said Davis was going to put tar on the Virginians' heels to make them stick and fight.

The Old North State is another nickname for North Carolina. Settlers divided the Carolina colony into two colonies in 1712. Settlers named the older northern colony North Carolina.

In the early 1600s, King Charles I ruled the land that became the North Carolina colony.

North Carolina adopted its state seal in 1893. The state seal reminds North Carolinians of their state's government. The seal also makes government papers official.

The center of North Carolina's state seal shows two female goddesses, Liberty and Ceres. Liberty stands for freedom and the state's government. Ceres stands for agriculture. Ceres sits next to a cornucopia full of fruit. The cornucopia stands for the large amount of crops grown in the state.

The scene behind Liberty and Ceres represents North Carolina's landscape and history. The state's mountains, plains, and coastline drew many settlers to the area. The ship stands for the state's shipbuilding and navy supply businesses.

North Carolina's state motto is "Esse Quam Videri." These Latin words mean "to be rather than to seem." North Carolinians believe in honesty.

North Carolina declared its independence from England on May 20, 1775. This date appears on the state seal.

State Capitol and Flag

North Carolina's capitol building is in Raleigh. Raleigh is the capital of North Carolina. Government officials work in the capitol to make the state's laws.

North Carolina has had three capitols. Fire destroyed the first building in 1798. Fire destroyed the second building in 1831. Builders completed the current capitol in 1840. The building cost $500,000.

Workers built the current capitol with granite mined from North Carolina quarries. The building has four wings that join in a round central room. This room is called a rotunda. A granite dome tops the rotunda.

North Carolina officials adopted the state flag in 1885. The left side of the flag is blue. The right side is red at the top and white at the bottom. Red and blue are North Carolina's state colors. A white star lies between a gold N and C on the flag's left side. These letters are North Carolina's initials.

A statue of Andrew Jackson, Andrew Johnson, and James K. Polk sits in front of the state capitol. These presidents were born in North Carolina.

State Bird

Officials chose the cardinal as North Carolina's state bird in 1943. Cardinals live in North Carolina all year. They are one of the most common birds in the state. These bright red birds were named after Roman Catholic cardinals. These priests wear bright red robes.

Male and female cardinals have different coloring. Male cardinals are bright red. They have black faces and short red bills. Female cardinals are brown. They have spots of red on their tails, wings, and heads. Their bills are pale red.

Cardinals eat mainly seeds. The birds crack seeds open easily with their strong bills. Cardinals also eat insects and worms.

Cardinals build nests in hidden spots in trees or bushes. The birds make nests with twigs, leaves, and weed stems. Female cardinals lay three or four white eggs with dark spots in their nests.

The cardinal's nickname is winter redbird because it is easily noticed in winter.

State Tree

In 1963, government officials named the longleaf pine as North Carolina's state tree. Longleaf pines grow throughout North Carolina. The tree is important to the state's timber business. People use the longleaf pine's strong wood to build furniture and houses.

Longleaf pines are evergreen trees. These trees are green year round. Longleaf pines have long, thin leaves called needles. The needles grow in bundles of three.

Longleaf pines grow slowly. Longleaf pines take from 200 to 400 years to grow to their full height. Most fully grown trees are 80 to 100 feet (24 to 30 meters) tall.

Longleaf pines have tall, straight trunks. The trunks also are thin. Fully grown trunks are only 24 to 32 inches (61 to 81 centimeters) wide.

North Carolina's early settlers used longleaf pine trees to build ships. The tall, thin trees made good masts.

State Flower

The blossom of the American dogwood tree became North Carolina's state flower in 1941. American dogwoods grow throughout North Carolina.

Flowering dogwood trees bloom from early spring to summer. The blossoms are 2 to 4 inches (5 to 10 centimeters) wide. Blossoms can be white or pink. Each blossom has a green-yellow center surrounded by four bracts. These brightly colored leaves look like petals. Many people enjoy the dogwood's sweet-smelling blossoms.

Blossoms fall off dogwood trees in early summer. Leaves and red berries grow in place of the blossoms. The oval leaves are 3 to 6 inches (8 to 15 centimeters) long. Each berry holds two seeds.

Flowering dogwoods are small trees. They grow 20 to 35 feet (6 to 11 meters) tall. Their trunks are 6 to 18 inches (15 to 46 centimeters) wide.

Each bract of a dogwood blossom has a V-shaped notch at its tip.

State Mammal

Officials made the gray squirrel North Carolina's state mammal in 1969. Gray squirrels live in North Carolina's cities and forests.

Gray squirrels are easy to recognize. They have gray fur. Their chests and stomachs are white. Squirrels have long, bushy tails. They use their tails to balance as they jump from tree to tree.

Gray squirrels eat insects, seeds, or nuts. The animals often live near trees that grow nuts. Gray squirrels bury many nuts in the ground in late summer and fall. Their strong sense of smell helps them find the buried nuts later.

In the fall, gray squirrels build leaf nests high in trees. Some build nests inside hollow tree trunks. Female squirrels usually give birth to four young squirrels. The young squirrels leave the nest when they are strong enough to live on their own.

Four sharp front teeth help gray squirrels bite through nut shells.

More State Symbols

State Dog: Officials made the Plott hound North Carolina's state dog in 1989. The Plott hound is the only dog breed native to North Carolina. Jonathan Plott developed the breed in 1750 to hunt wild boars.

State Gemstone: Officials made the emerald the state gemstone in 1973. Emeralds look like pieces of bright green glass. Miners have found many large and valuable emeralds in North Carolina.

State Reptile: The eastern box turtle became the state reptile in 1979. Box turtles eat plants and insects that damage crops.

State Shell: The Scotch bonnet has been North Carolina's state shell since 1965. This cream-colored shell has orange and tan blocks like Scottish plaid.

State Vegetable: North Carolina schoolchildren chose the sweet potato as the state vegetable in 1995. North Carolina is the largest producer of sweet potatoes in the United States.

Orange and red blotches cover the eastern box turtle's dark brown shell.

Places to Visit

Blue Ridge Parkway

The Blue Ridge Parkway is in the Appalachian Mountains. This scenic drive is 469 miles (755 kilometers) long. Visitors drive through the curving mountain passes. At stopping places, they hike past waterfalls and wildlife. Visitors also walk across a high swinging bridge between two mountain peaks.

Paramount's Carowinds Theme Park

Paramount's Carowinds Theme Park is in Charlotte. The park has more than 40 rides, shows, and attractions. Visitors swim and go on water rides in the park's WaterWorks area. Carowinds also has 11 areas with different themes about North or South Carolina.

Wright Brothers National Historic Site

The Wright Brothers National Historic Site is in Kill Devil Hills. Wilbur and Orville Wright made the world's first successful airplane flight here in 1903. The site features exhibits and full-scale models of the brothers' planes.

Words to Know

bract (BRAKT)—a colorful leaf; dogwood blossoms have four bracts that look like petals.

colony (KAHL-uh-nee)—land governed by another country; a group of people who leave their own country to settle in a colony are called colonists.

cornucopia (kore-nuh-KOH-pee-uh)—a horn-shaped container for food; this symbol stands for plenty.

plaid (PLAD)—a pattern of squares in cloth formed by weaving stripes of different widths and colors that cross each other

quarry (KWAHR-ee)—a place where workers cut or blast stone out of the ground

Read More

Bock, Judy and Rachel Kranz. *Scholastic Encyclopedia of the United States.* New York: Scholastic, 1997.

Hintz, Martin and Stephen Hintz. *North Carolina.* America the Beautiful. New York: Children's Press, 1998.

Joseph, Paul. *North Carolina.* United States. Minneapolis: Abdo & Daughters, 1998.

Kummer, Patricia K. *North Carolina.* One Nation. Mankato, Minn.: Capstone Press, 1998.

Useful Addresses

North Carolina Division of Tourism
301 North Wilmington Street
Raleigh, NC 27626

North Carolina Secretary of State
300 North Salisbury Street
Raleigh, NC 27603-5909

Internet Sites

Geobop's North Carolina Symbols
http://www.geobop.com/Eco/NC.htm
North Carolina Kids Page
http://www.state.nc.us./secstate/kidspg/kids.htm
Stately Knowledge
http://www.ipl.org/youth/stateknow/nc1.html
Wright Brothers National Historic Site
http://www.nps.gov/wrbr/wb_safety.htm

Index